I0746449

Frank Mercer
In

THE
MERCER
FILES

The Murder of the Silent Man

Phillip Deam

Introduction:

There's a cold truth in this line of work.
People don't call a private eye when life's going right.

They call when something's rotting under the floorboards.

When the smiles are fake.

When the bank accounts are empty.

When the lies pile high enough to block out daylight.

This time, it was a rich family out on the edge of town.

A house big enough to hold a hundred secrets.
Marble floors, silk curtains, polished silver.
But money doesn't keep the rot out.

They told me the old man died of natural causes.
Fell asleep at his desk, glass in hand, papers still spread in front of him.

But when you've been around as many bodies as I
have, you start to know: nothing about death is ever
natural.

They wanted me to poke around,
make sure the paperwork lined up,
quiet any doubts before the lawyers got involved.
The minute I walked through that door,
I knew.

There was more here than they wanted me to see.
And before the night was over,
I'd know exactly how deep the rot ran.

Chapter 1:
Whispers and Wallpaper

Money builds big houses. Secrets keep the lights low

Frank Mercer

Rain hits this city like a debt collector, heavy, loud, and overdue. Just another night in this godforsaken city.

Rich areas or poor, it's always the same: death, money, and broads. And this time, the dead man had a view, a study full of books, a decanter full of top-shelf lies, and a family with secrets thicker than the city fog.

The city keeps its secrets well, tucked into shadows, hidden under silk sheets, or buried six feet under. But if you know where to look, sometimes you can pry a few loose.

Rita sent me out tonight. A call to the outer edges of the city, out where the mansions sit heavy on their acres and the air smells like old money and fresh lies.

Not my usual beat, but the pay was good, and I've learned that in places like this, money can buy silence, but it sure as hell can't buy innocence.

I pull up in the battered Plymouth, engine coughing smoke and steam under the polished awning of the estate.

A tall man, stretched thin like someone had pulled him too hard from both ends, steps forward and opens the door.

"Welcome, Mr. Mercer," he says, voice slow, a little too smooth. "I'm Mr. Sloan, the keeper of the manor."

I slide out, flicking the last drag off my Lucky Strike into the wet night, grinding it under my heel.

"Mr. Appleby Junior is expecting you," Sloan says, drawing out every word like they cost him extra breath. "Please wait in the lobby. I shall take you through shortly."

Inside, the place was just what you'd expect. Marble floors that gleamed too clean, oil paintings watching from the walls, everything polished to the point of hiding the blood beneath.

I pace the lobby, with sharp eyes scanning every corner.

The silence stretched.

A few minutes later, Sloan returns, his oversized suit hanging off his stretched frame, as he gestures.

"Mr. Appleby Jr. will see you now."

Mr. Sloan led me down a long hall, soft carpet underfoot, thick enough to bury secrets in. He opened the heavy oak door to the office… no, the lounge, and it was everything you'd expect from a man with money: dark wood paneling, walls lined with leather-bound books, glass decanters catching the dim light, the faint smell of old smoke and older deals.

Mr. Appleby Jr. sat behind a wide mahogany desk, polished to a shine. He gestured for me to sit without standing, lifting the lid of the cigar box near his elbow.

"Cigar, Mr. Mercer?"

I offered a small grin.
Who was I to turn down a high-end cigar?

"Don't mind if I do," I said, taking one and rolling it between my fingers before lighting up.

The room filled with the rich smell of exotic tobaccos, spice, leather, a hit of pepper. A guy could get used to this.

"So, Mr. Mercer, did your… receptionist explain why you're here?"
I gave a slow shrug. No need to hand him everything upfront.

"A little. But why don't you tell me again?"

"My father, Mr. Appleby Senior, was found dead in his study yesterday.

The officers called it natural causes. No signs of foul play, no need to investigate further, they said.

But… my mother, Mrs. Appleby, she's not convinced. She wants someone to look into it. I… I don't know why. To me, it seems like a waste of time, but here we are."

"No wounds on the body? Nothing suspicious?"

"No. He was found slumped over his desk. No blood, no signs of a struggle. Just… gone."
"And enemies? Any reason someone would want your father dead?"

He sighed. "My father… was a successful businessman. Not a great father, mind you, but he knew how to build an empire. You don't get to the top without making a few enemies, I suppose."

His eyes shifted, "Though… there's something you should know."
My gaze narrowed through the cigar smoke.

"My father lost his ability to speak several years ago. An accident. He fell down the stairs, hit his head hard. Since then… nothing."

"Couldn't muster a word."

His thumb ran back and forth along his jaw line.

"So, if he was worried about anything, if there was something on his mind, he couldn't tell anyone."

I tapped the ash of my cigar.

"I suppose him falling down the stairs was… an accident as well?"

Mr. Appleby Jr. shifted in his chair, "Are you asking if someone pushed him, Mr. Mercer? I… I hadn't considered that. He was just found at the bottom of the staircase. Some blood from the back of his head, broken arm. The doctors said he was lucky to survive at all."

"Lucky, sure." Lucky enough to keep living, but not lucky enough to keep talking. And now here I am, hired to look into his death because someone in this house thinks lightning struck twice.

"Alright, first things first, I want to see the study where he was found."

"Then I'll need to meet everyone who lives here, family, staff, anyone with access to Mr. Appleby Senior."

"Of course. I'll have Mr. Sloan take you through. You'll want to speak with my mother, the nurse, Mr. Sloan and of course, myself and my sister."

A house this size, this clean, hides its sins well.

But the thing about secrets is, they don't stay
hidden for long when you start poking in the right
places.

I watched Appleby Jr. across the desk, sharp suit,
clean nails, no rough edges.
A man born into money, not a man who fought for
it.

His eyes flicked to the decanter on the sideboard
more than once during our talk, but he never got up
to pour a drink. Nerves?

Or just used to someone else handling the bottle for
him?

I let the silence hang a beat too long, watching how
he shifted in it. People tell you plenty when you let
them sit with their own thoughts.

Finally, he cleared his throat, straightened up.

"Will you help us, Mr. Mercer?"

I ground out the last of the cigar, gave him a slow
nod.

"I'll look into it. I'd like to start with the study, where
they found the body. Then I'll want to meet
everyone who was here. Family or otherwise."

Money, mystery, and a family full of silk gloves and hidden knives. This wasn't just a case. This was a storm dressed like a dinner party.

Chapter 2:
A Family Built on Silence

Blood runs thicker than whiskey — but it stains the same.

Frank Mercer

Mr. Sloan led me down a long, polished corridor, the kind where your footsteps echo too loud and the air feels thick with old money and old ghosts.

We stopped at a heavy wooden door near the end. Sloan, all stretched limbs and deliberate slowness, reached out and eased it open, his arm extending like a dark branch.

"Here we are, Mr. Mercer," he said, voice dragging like syrup. He raised that long arm slightly, inviting me in with the kind of theatrical flourish you'd expect from a stage butler.

"I can take it from here, Stretch."

Sloan gave the faintest tip of his head, the corners of his mouth just twitching at the nickname.

"As you wish, Mr. Mercer," he said, before turning to leave.

"Wait, Mr. Sloan."

The butler stopped, pivoting back slightly.

"Yes, Mr. Mercer?" His voice, long and drawn.

"Who found the body?"

Sloan blinked slowly, as if the memory itself had to pull itself up from deep storage.

"It was… the nurse, sir. Miss Claire. She was delivering Mr. Appleby's evening medications."

"And what time was that?"

He tilted his head slightly. "Around half-past eight, sir. I was in the east wing at the time… assisting Mrs. Appleby."

I gave a slow nod, eyes flicking over the man's composed expression, filing that detail away. A nurse found the body. A wife in another wing. A son who wasn't sure why I was even here.

Yeah… this place was going to be interesting.

I stepped into the study, shoes sinking softly into the heavy rug, eyes sweeping the room.
First thing that hit me: The desk.
Immaculate.

Not a single paper out of place, not a speck of dust on the surface.

For a room where a man supposedly died less than twenty-four hours ago, it was too clean.

Like someone had been through here with a fine-tooth comb, tidying up before I could get my hands on the scene.

On the desk, just the essentials: a fine cigar box, a silver lighter, and a decanter half-filled with what smelled like an expensive scotch, deep, oaky, the kind of drink you savor, not slug back.

I gave it a slow swirl under my nose. A man with taste, even if the taste didn't keep him breathing. My eyes drifted to the bookshelf.

Just because a man couldn't speak didn't mean he didn't have anything to say. Could've left a note, a diary, a warning tucked where no one thought to look.

I pulled a few books from the shelves, gave them a shake. Nothing.
Tried a few more, still nothing.

Not yet, anyway.

I went for the obvious spots next: under the desk, the file cabinet, the drawers.
In the middle drawer, my fingers brushed something odd, a false bottom.

Hidden compartment.

I pried it up, careful, slow… but it was already empty.

Either it was an old stash, long forgotten, or someone else knew about it and got here before me.

I opened the cigar box, thinking maybe I'd help myself to a celebratory smoke when this was all wrapped up.

The box was down to the last row.
But as I lifted one cigar, something caught my eye.

A slip of paper tucked just beneath.

Fine penmanship.
Dark ink.
Looked like a letter.

I slipped it out slowly, holding it up to the light, heart beating just a little faster.

Maybe the dead still had something to say.

I pulled the letter from the box, fingers brushing the delicate paper, but before I could read a word,

Footsteps. Heavy, quick, coming down the hall.
I pocketed the letter fast, hoping to read it somewhere a little more private.

A short, stumpy blonde woman bustled into the room, nearly colliding with me.

"Oh! Excuse me," she said, blinking up at me. "Who are you, and what are you doing in Mr. Appleby's study?"

I tipped my hat slightly, giving her the kind of smile that rarely reached my eyes.

"Frank Mercer, ma'am. I'm looking into the death of the old man."

Her eyes widened just a touch.

"Oh… but the police said it was just natural causes."

"And you are?" I asked, voice smooth, but the weight behind it was clear.

"Oh, I'm Nurse Buckley," she said, straightening a little, brushing at her apron.

"I've been with Mr. Appleby ever since his… unfortunate accident on the stairs. After that, I stayed on to help with his medications, make sure everything was in order."

I raised my eyebrow as I started to speak. "Ah, yes, the 'accident' down the stairs," I said, letting the sarcasm drip off the words.

"Tell me, Nurse Buckley, who found the body?"

She tapped a finger against her lips, thinking.

"Oh, I believe Miss Appleby, the daughter. She found her father here yesterday morning."

"Is that so? And when was the last time you saw the old man?"

I pulled out my pack of Lucky Strikes, shuffling it in my palm, flicking the bottom till one slid forward. Let it hang on my lip, eyes fixed on her.

"Ah… let me think… oh yes," she said, perking up. "I gave him his medicine the night before. Six-thirty sharp, like clockwork."

"And where was he when you saw him?" I asked, voice low, watching her closely.

"Oh, he was in the library, reading the newspaper."

"I see."

I looked up at her, keeping my expression neutral. "Got a light?"

Without missing a beat, Nurse Buckley moved through the study like she owned the place. She went straight to the bottom drawer of Mr. Appleby's desk. She fished out a fancy cigar lighter, passing it across to me, disregarding the one on the desk. She knew her way around the office well, for a nurse.

The flame nearly singed my eyebrows off, but it did the job. I breathed deep, holding the smoke a little longer than necessary.

"Tell me, Nurse Buckley, what's it like working here?"

Her hands folded nervously.

"It's been a pleasure, most of the time, Mr. Mercer." She placed her left hand on her hip as she spoke.

"It's just… sometimes, it's a bit tense, you know… with Miss Appleby and her brother."

She leaned in slightly, voice dropping just a notch.

"You didn't hear this from me, but… I think I heard that Mr. Appleby was going to take them out of the will."

"He couldn't talk, Nurse.
So how'd you hear that?"

She took a small pause.
Her hands smoothed the front of her knee-length skirt.

"Oh… uh, I think I heard Mrs. Appleby talking about
it. Yes. She was… um… mentioned it."

"Yeah?"
My left eyebrow raised.
The creases deepened in my brow.
"And who was she talking to about that?"

"Oh, I… I couldn't speak to that, Mr. Mercer.
I truly have no idea."

"Uh-huh."
A pause too long.
Jaw too tight.

People never like to lie to my face.

But they do it anyway.

And when they do, I know there's more to dig up.

That story had more holes than a cheap trench
coat.

So far, two people, two different stories, and not a
single alibi offered.

I reached up, softened the tie around my neck.
It didn't help.
It never does.

My mouth twitched in the right corner before I spoke.

"Tell me, Nurse, where can I find Miss Appleby?"

"Oh… she'll be in the main wing at this time of night," she said, voice lowering slightly.

"Music and champagne, I believe."

"Hey, Nurse…"

My thumb rolled across the crown of my father's wrist watch.

"Yes, Mr. Mercer?"

"Don't go packing your things just yet."

Her eyes widened a touch, surprise flickering across her face before she spun and hurried down the hallway.

I smirked faintly.

Now how the hell do I find the main wing?

I wandered back down the corridor, ears pricking as the faint crackle of music floated through the air. Piano jazz.

The closer I got, the louder the scratchy record grew, crackling under the needle of the gramophone. I figured if I just followed the noise, I'd eventually find someone worth talking to.

I stepped through a wide, arched entry, no door, just a carved opening that led into a larger, open room.

Like the rest of the house, it was sterile, polished to within an inch of its life. A place so pristine it felt more like a museum exhibit than a home, everything perfect on the surface, and none of it real.

And there she was.

Miss Appleby.

Maybe thirty, golden wavy hair cascading down her shoulders, wearing a flowing pale-gold silk dress that clung just enough to hint at danger.

Over it, a dramatic, fluffy shawl; the kind of thing only someone rich enough to ignore practicality would throw on.

She floated across the floor, spinning gently, arms lifted, lost in the haze of champagne and scratchy piano music.

She looked like an angel dipped in gold, gliding across the room… and there I was, all trenchcoat and cigarette smoke.

I cleared my throat softly.

She paused mid-turn, noticing me for the first time, a shy smile curling at the corners of her lips.

"Oh my… I'm sorry, sir. I didn't see you there."

We introduced ourselves, her voice soft and musical as she sipped her champagne, smiling faintly over the rim of the glass.

"Can I offer you a drink, Mr. Mercer?" she asked, eyes glinting playfully.
A grin came across my face, the kind that didn't reach my eyes.
"Bourbon, if you have it."

She glided across the room like an angel, sent by God himself. Carrying bourbon instead of salvation. She poured a glass with delicate care and handed it to me, her fingers brushing mine.

"So… how's the investigation going?" she asked, tilting her head, curls slipping over her shoulder.

"Nothing solid yet."

I took a slow sip, letting the warmth spread down my throat.
"Can I ask you a few questions, Miss Appleby?"

"Oh yes, please do," she said, placing a soft hand on my arm.

It caught me by surprise, a touch that lingered just a little too long, a glint in her eyes that wasn't all innocence.
There was something off here…
A hint of danger, the kind a man could get himself lost in.

"Do you know who found the body?"

She took another sip, swaying slightly to the music.

"Oh yes… I heard Mother say that my brother found the body, around lunchtime on Tuesday. He was going to try to discuss a new business venture.
Poor fellow, he walked in and found Father slumped on his desk."

My brow arched slightly.
A third timeline.
What the hell was going on in this household?

"How was your relationship with your father?"

Her head dipped a little.
"Oh, he was a sweet man. A cunning businessman,

but a sweet man.
It was heartbreaking when he had his accident
down the stairs…"

"Oh yeah… the accident."

Her eyes sharpened just a touch.
"Excuse me, Mr. Mercer… what do you mean by
that?"

I coughed lightly, taking one last drag from my
Lucky Strike, flicking the ash aside.
"Nothing at all, Miss Appleby."

"Tell me, how was your brother's relationship with
your father?"

She sighed faintly, gaze drifting.

"Oh… strained, at the best of times. After the
accident, it only got worse. Without Father's ability
to speak, everything just… soured. He grew more
paranoid by the day."

"Paranoid, you say?"

"Oh yes… but why, I couldn't say."
Her soft lips touched the crystal champagne flute
as she spoke.
"He became a recluse after the accident,
separating himself from us one by one.
I do miss my dear father."

I thanked her for her time.

My thoughts ticking.

I rubbed my thumb along my jaw.

Another timeline.

Another lie wrapped in silk and sin.

Another set of tangled threads.
But before I could slip away,

"Would you like to dance, Mr. Mercer?"
I paused.
Just one, I told myself.

"Sure thing, baby girl."

I put my arms around her waist, pulling her in close.
She smelled divine, sweet and light, like something
heaven forgot to take back.

But I'd been around long enough to know.
Even angels cast shadows.

After the dance, I slipped away, making polite
excuses and heading down the hall to the guest
room they'd set aside for me.

My door closed, coat off.

My father's worn down old silver coin flipped slowly
across my knuckles. Catching the glint of the lamp
with each turn.

I pulled the letter from my pocket and unfolded it
carefully.

The penmanship was impeccable, tight, elegant
loops of ink flowing across the page.

The only problem?
It was written as a poem.

I flipped the coin in the air.

Caught it without breaking my concentration on the
note.

A locked door behind velvet hands,
The gold-toothed smile, the shifting sands.
A son who whispers, a daughter who weeps,
A secret the widow intends to keep.
The bottle's last drop, the final breath,
A silent room, a sudden death.
Seek the shadow that walks at night,
Behind the glass, beyond the light.

I stared at the lines.
Flipped the coin again.

I had no damn idea what it meant, or if it even had anything to do with the old man's death.

But something told me… it mattered.

And I'd better figure it out before someone else decides to help me join the old man in the family ledger.

I slipped the letter back into my coat pocket. Cryptic. Clearly about the son and daughter, but it hinted at a secret, maybe something the old man had seen.

I knocked back the last of my bourbon, savoring the heat, and decided to head back to the study. Maybe I'd missed something.

On the way, I nearly collided with her, Mrs. Appleby.

Elderly, sure, but still pretty in her own right, sharp features, slim frame, hair pulled back tight even this late hour.
But there was something in her eyes… tired, withdrawn.
Like a woman stretched thin from years of balancing grace over grief.

"Mrs. Appleby, I presume."
She offered a weary smile.

"Yes… and you must be Mr. Mercer.
Thank you so much for coming. I feel… safer
knowing you're here."

"You imply you're not safe here alone, Mrs.
Appleby. Care to elaborate?"

She gave a quiet, delicate laugh, shaking her head
slightly.
"Oh, no… no. I just… I miss my husband." She
stood uneasily at the remark.

"It's just nice to have a man roaming the house
again, even under these circumstances."

I let the silence hang for a moment,
"Can you tell me, Mrs. Appleby, who found the
body?"

"Oh yes, Mr. Mercer,
I believe it was Mr. Sloan who found the body in the
study."

Of course it was.
Another answer, another timeline.
I was starting to get a little frustrated with the lack
of consistency, or maybe just the sheer number of
tangled stories I was being fed.

"Can you tell me, Mrs. Appleby, how's the house
been since 'the accident'?"

She smoothed her hands down her skirt, giving a
faint but practiced smile.
"Oh, it's been fine, sir." Her gaze returned to meet
mine.

"We're just a happy family, no real troubles…
just the occasional bickering, as you might find
anywhere."

Uh-huh.
A happy family.
And I'm the Easter Bunny.

"Any idea what might've happened to the old
man… if it wasn't natural causes, that is?"

She hesitated, just slightly.

"Oh, no, Mr. Mercer. My husband…
My husband had his enemies. He was a shrewd
businessman, but most of his ventures dissipated
after the accident. To my knowledge, we're barely
holding on."

"Did your husband keep a ledger somewhere?"

"Yes," she nodded faintly, tapping a delicate finger
against her lips.
"I believe it's in a drawer of his study desk."

The second drawer, I thought.

The one with the hidden compartment, the one I'd
already found emptied out.

If the ledger was gone, it wasn't an accident.
It was cleaned out, and it likely showed something
none of them wanted seen:
a fortune dwindling away, piece by piece.

"Thank you, Mrs. Appleby.
If I have any more questions, I'll find you in the
morning."

She gave a faint, brittle smile.

"Of course, Mr. Mercer.
Good night."

Chapter 3:
The Ledger and the Lie

The truth's like cheap bourbon, the longer it sits, the harder it burns.

Frank Mercer

I made my way down the hall, shoes soft on the thick carpet, when I spotted him.

Mr. Sloan. Tall, stretched out, just stepping out of the study, quietly pulling the door closed behind him.

"Mr. Mercer… I'm surprised you're still awake at this hour," he said with his drawn out tone.

"Oh, I'm just a bit of a night owl, Mr. Sloan. Figured I'd check the study one last time while everyone's off to sleep."

Sloan gave a measured nod.
"Ah… I see. If you'll excuse me, Sir. I still have my rounds to finish."

I paused for a moment. "Mr. Sloan."

"Yes?"

"Would there be something to drink in the office? Bourbon, perhaps?"

Sloan allowed himself a small smile.
"Yes, Mr. Mercer. Mr. Appleby kept a fine selection in the cupboard next to the bookshelf."

I gave a slight nod as he drifted away down the
hall.

Pushed the door open, and flicked the light switch.

The study lit up softly, the warm glow washing over
the books, the decanter, the polished desk.

But something…
Something was off.

Not by much, no overturned chairs, no smashed
glass, but the air felt skewed.

Just a hair off balance.

If this were my first time stepping into the room, I'd
say it was perfect, immaculate, like the rest of the
house.

But I'd been here before.
And now?

My mind buzzed on edge.

I instinctively pulled at my cuffs.

Stay sharp, Frank.

Mrs. Appleby said the ledger was in the second
drawer.
Let's check that first.

I slid the drawer open, slow.
It gave a faint creak, heavy and solid, like old bones
shifting under too much weight.

Empty.

I reached carefully, fingers feeling along the bottom,
then slipped under the false panel.
And there it was.

Like it had been waiting for me,
The ledger.

Pulled from hiding like a secret waiting just for me.

I set the green ledger down on the desk, the leather
cracked and worn, the corners softened by years of
quiet hands. Moving to the cabinet Sloan had
mentioned, I gave the door a tug, it creaked open
like an old man's sigh.

No Beam, Just Tavern.

Figures.

This house was lousy for bourbon, but there were a
few other decent bottles tucked away.

I didn't bother with the sniff test, just poured three
fingers into a glass and set it next to the ledger.

I flipped open the book, eyes narrowing.

A lot of question marks.
Black ink.

Seventeen entries, each a neat $5,000 withdrawal,
all marked on the 3rd of the month, each circled in
red with a sharp, irritated hand.

Pages had been ripped out, no finesse, just torn
free.

I sipped my drink, rolling the warmth down my
throat, and tried to make sense of it.
Toward the back, things got… stranger.

Three inks now, black, red, blue, each marking
separate withdrawals, layered like competing
voices.

At the bottom of the pages, coded lines.
Snippets of the poem, scrawled in the same three
colors as the question marks.

The bottle's last drop and the final breath, written in
black.

A silent room and a sudden death, written in blue.

A secret the widow intends to keep. And behind the
glass, beyond the light written in red.

My brow hardened as I studied the text.

The handwriting changed.
A sharper, urgent style:
Seek the shadow that walks at night.

The old man knew.
He knew he was dying.
He knew someone was trying to kill him.
He just didn't know who would get there first.

I sat at the desk, fingers tapping lightly on the leather cover of the green ledger.
Footsteps. I stayed alert, but relaxed, shoulders loose, eyes half-lidded as the sound drew closer.

The door creaked open, and there she was.

Miss Appleby.
She drifted into the room in silk nightwear, the silhouette of her body sharp against the dim light, captivating, magnetic.

"Oh, Mr. Mercer… what are you doing in Father's study?" she asked, voice soft, almost breathless.

"Just some quiet reading," I said, tapping the ledger with one finger.

"Oh… oh, I see…"
She moved closer, hips swaying as she crossed the room, her golden hair spilling over one bare shoulder.

Under my breath, I murmured,
"Like God had sent her Himself."

"What was that, Mr. Mercer?" she asked, tilting her
head with a teasing smile.

I took a slow sip of bourbon, eyes glinting.
"Nothing, baby doll."

She reached down, fingers brushing my stubbled
cheek, caressing lightly.

"Do you really think…
Someone tried to hurt my father?" she whispered.

I looked up at her from the old man's leather chair,
steady, certain.

"Baby girl," I said softly.
"I've never been more sure of anything in my life."
She gasped softly, but her hand never left my face.
In the back of my mind, the ledger's notes were
starting to click into place.

"Would you like a nightcap, Miss Appleby."

I felt a faint flush rise to my cheeks as I said it.

She didn't blink.

Just held my gaze.

Her golden hair bounced lightly as she nodded.

"Sure."

I stepped over to the cabinet, pulled out a glass,
and poured from the decanter on the desk,
just for her.
I had to know.
One way or the other.

Her expression went soft as she took a sip.

Okay, not her.
I gave a small grin, shaking my head.

"I think that glass was dusty. Let me pour
something different."

I handed her a new drink and drifted to the window.

The stars stretched wide above the estate, clear
and bright, a sky completely different from the city.
Less smog.
Less grime.

Same bad intentions.

I stared through the window, watching the stars
scatter across the countryside sky, my thoughts

spinning tight.

Slowly, I circled back around the room.

Miss Appleby sat quietly by the fireplace, sipping
from her glass, the soft golden shimmer of her silk
gown catching the low light.
She looked like an angel.
But maybe…

Maybe an angel of death.

Time would tell.

My eyes caught on something I'd missed before,
a small, wall-mounted cabinet, just beside the liquor
cabinet.

"Is there a key for this?" I asked, glancing over my
shoulder.

She tilted her head, smiling faintly.
"Yes, Mr. Mercer… but you'll need to ask the nurse
for it. She's the only one who has it."

"Medicine, I assume?"

"Yes, Mr. Mercer," she murmured, voice soft, eyes
glinting faintly as she sipped again from her glass.

I took another slow sip of bourbon, eyes narrowing
slightly.

The nurse.
The locked cabinet.
The medicine no one else touched.

Suddenly, the pieces weren't just floating anymore.
They were beginning to fall into place.

"Have you read this ledger before?" I asked,
tapping the worn green cover, eyes flicking up to
the golden-haired goddess across the room.

She gave a soft, wistful stare, brushing a loose curl
behind her ear.

"To my shame, Mr. Mercer… Yes, I have."
Her head dropped a little.

"But I couldn't make heads or tails of it.
Just a lot of babble in the margins, strange marks…
and a lot of missing pages.
I'm sure there's nothing in there that's helpful
anymore."

Uh-huh.
That's what they always say… right before you find
the piece they hoped was buried.

My mouth lifted from one corner, leaning back
slightly in the chair.

"Alright, baby girl.
Can you bring the decanter and some glasses
down to the library, please?"

She tilted her head slightly, golden hair catching the
low light.

"Yes, Mr. Mercer…
Is everything okay?"

I offered a slow, easy grin, the kind that never
reached my eyes.

"Everything's fine, baby girl."

Chapter 4:
The Night the House Spoke

By the time truth shows up, everyone's already sides.
Even the dead.

Frank Mercer

We gathered in the library, drinks in hand, eyes
flicking from face to face.
Mr. Sloan stood by the door, posture tall and
careful.

Mrs. Appleby sat by the fireplace, a faint crease in
her brow.

The son, arms folded, tense.

The nurse, alert, watchful, like she was ready to
cuff someone if she had to.

And Miss Appleby…
Well, she floated like she always did, a glass
resting delicately between her fingers, golden hair
catching the lamplight.

I raised my glass to the room.

"Cheers, everyone.
To family.
To this fine house.
And to the finest scotch I've ever tasted,"

I watched them sip.

"Straight from the old man's decanter."

I grinned as I said it, waiting for one of them
to react.

Mr. Appleby Jr. started sputtering and coughed it back into his glass.

"You alright?" I asked softly.

"I'm fine," he muttered, shaking his head. "I … I never cared for Father's scotch. It reminds me too much of him. Saddens me."

"Sure it does, kid."

I set my glass down and stepped forward.

I reached into my coat pocket and pulled out the folded note from the cigar box.

The room went quiet.

Even the fire seemed to settle.

I unfolded the paper slowly.

"Found this in your father's study."

My eyes drifted across the room.

"He couldn't speak anymore."

I glanced toward the old man's son.

"But that doesn't mean he had nothing to say."

I cleared my throat and read.

"A locked door behind velvet hands."

My gaze found Mrs. Appleby.

"The gold-toothed smile, the shifting sands."

Mr. Appleby Jr. stared at the floor.

"A son who whispers, a daughter who weeps."

Miss Appleby's grip tightened around her glass.

"A secret the widow intends to keep."

Nobody spoke.

Nobody moved.

"The bottle's last drop. The final breath."

I let the words hang.

"A silent room. A sudden death."

The room felt smaller now.

Like the walls were leaning in.

I folded the note carefully.

"At first I thought it was a riddle."

I shook my head.

"It wasn't."

"It was a record."

"A man trying to tell the truth after his voice had already been taken from him."

My thumb rubbed along the edge of the paper.

"The old man knew."

"He knew money was disappearing."

"He knew somebody was poisoning his whiskey."

"He knew his medications weren't helping."

My eyes drifted slowly around the room.

"And somewhere along the way..."

I paused.

"I think he remembered what really happened on those stairs."

Silence.

Heavy silence.

"Maybe he figured it out too late."

"Maybe he spent years trying to work out which one of you would get there first."

I folded the note and slid it back into my pocket.

"Turns out he didn't have to."

"You all did."

I let the silence settle over the room.

Watched them.

The son couldn't sit still.

The nurse wouldn't look at me.

Miss Appleby held her glass a little tighter than
before.

Funny thing about guilt.

It always wants to be noticed.

I reached into my coat pocket and pulled out
the battered pack of cigarettes.

Only two left.

I smirked slightly, and looked up at them.
"Maybe today's the day I quit."

I flicked the bottom, popped the second last
one through the foil, set it between my lips,
and held the flame a second longer than I
needed, just long enough to make them
sweat.

I inhaled deep, savoring the taste, the
moment while they sat there in silence,
avoiding eye contact.

They say the rich are different from the poor,
but when you peel back the skin, it's the
same bones underneath: greed, betrayal,
and the kind of love that eats you alive.

"Please, Mr. Mercer, what does all this
mean?" said the voice of an angel from
across the room.

A small twitch at the side of my mouth.

"Mr. Appleby Jr. was slipping poison into his
father's whiskey. Furious over bad business
deals, desperate after his father refused to
bail him out, quietly siphoning money from
the accounts."

My voice, coarse now from cigarettes.

"You weren't trying to kill him, not at first,
 you just wanted to keep him weak, under
your thumb. But it chipped away at him, piece
by piece."

I took a slow pull from my cigarette.

Let the smoke dance through the room.

Moved my attention to the nurse and Mrs.
Appleby.

"And you, Mrs. Appleby,
with the nurse at your side, adjusting
medications, upping doses, changing
prescriptions."

I swirled the whisky around the glass as I
spoke.
"Why?"

"Because the old man was worth more dead
than alive."

Mrs. Appleby's head sank. An admission of
guilt in any language.

"You needed the insurance money. You said
it yourself; you were barely hanging on
financially."

"Every night you tucked him in; I bet you told
yourself you were just…
helping nature along."

My gaze drifted to the girl who should have
been his salvation.

Instead

His was his sharpest betrayal.

"His golden child."

"The one he trusted, right up until the fog lifted from his concussion, and he remembered it was *you* who bumped him down the stairs."

Her eyes dropped from my stare.

"You, the one quietly draining assets from the family trust, selling off pieces behind his back. And the heartbreak you dealt him. That was the final nail."

A soft sob from behind her hands covering her face.

"You didn't need poison or pills, baby girl, you broke him from the inside out."

"Just like you do to every man in your life."

Staying calm in my moment,
"The only decent one among you…
was the shadow who walked at night."

"Mr. Sloan.
The man who slipped the ledger back where it belonged."

"The man who saw the truth but stayed silent, confiding only in the one person no one else was listening to."

Mr. Sloan stood tall, proud.

And if you check the will, I think you'll find…
the old man left the estate to the only person
who tried to help him."

I watched their faces.

No denials.

No gasps.

Just the slow, sinking realization that they'd
all played a part, unbeknownst to each other.

Not one killer, but a whole web of betrayals,
each tightening the noose until the old man
couldn't breathe anymore.

"You didn't just kill a man.
You killed a family."

"And the funny thing is, you'll all have to live
with that longer than any sentence the law
could hand down."

The room sat heavy in silence.
No one moved.
No one spoke.

Just the soft ticking of the clock over the
fireplace, marking the last moments of a
family's crumbling empire.

I flicked the stub of my cigarette into the
fireplace, watching the ember spark out.

I adjusted my coat, smoothed my hat down,
and turned to the door.

As I reached the threshold, I paused just long
enough to toss one last glance over my
shoulder.

"Don't worry, folks…
I still send invoices."

And with that, I walked out.

Coat collar high.

Shoes echoing down the polished hall.

Leaving behind the quiet ruin of a house that
had already torn itself apart.

I stood at the step, under the front awning
where it all started.

I lit the last lucky, smirked at it a little, maybe
today would be the day I quit.

Final Thoughts:

I left them sitting there, a room full of polished ghosts. No handcuffs. No police. Just the truth, laid bare like an open wound.

They didn't need a judge or jury; they were already trapped, caught in the quiet punishment of knowing they'd all helped kill the one man holding their world together.

That's the funny thing about the rich. They think they're different. But strip away the suits, the diamonds, the polished silver and underneath.

Same old cracked hearts, same old desperate lies, same old endings.

I stepped into the night, cold air biting against my skin. Another name scratched off the list, another case closed, another ghost filed away.

At the end of the day, there's only one guarantee in this business: You follow the truth wherever it leads, and if you're lucky, you walk away with just enough left to send an invoice.

Thank you for your support

If you've made it this far, you've got a stronger stomach than most folks in this city.

Thanks for stepping into the shadows with me and digging through the lies.

If you're hungry for more cases, or you want to hear my voice telling it like it is, come join me on YouTube at:
www.youtube.com/@TheMercerFiles

Hit that like and subscribe button, helps keep the lights on and the bourbon flowing.*

Or if you're the kind who likes to peek behind the curtain and support these investigations even deeper, swing by my Patreon page:
https://www.patreon.com/c/TheMercerFiles

Feel Free to "Buy Me a Coffee" from
coff.ee/TheMercerFiles

Stay tuned for the next case file.

Some stories don't end. They just wait for the next page.

Watch the full episode on our
Youtube channel by scanning the
QR code below.

www.ingramcontent.com/pod-product-compliance
Lightning Source LLC
Chambersburg PA
CBHW040235170726
48295CB00014B/930